How to Play Ten-Pin Bowling

Cameron Macintosh

Photographs by Lindsay Edwards

Contents

Goal

To knock over the most **pins**, with a heavy ball

Materials

You will need:

- a bowling **lane**

- bowling shoes

- a bowling ball.

You will need some family or friends to play with, too.

Steps

1. Before you start playing,
put your bowling shoes on.
They will help you not to slip and fall
in the bowling lane.

Check that your shoes are done up tightly.

2. Find a bowling ball that is right for you.
Your ball should not be too heavy or too light.

A bowling ball has holes that help you hold on to it.
Your fingers need to fit in the holes, but not too tightly.

3. Before you bowl, put one hand under the ball. Then, put the thumb of your other hand in the biggest hole on the ball.

Put your two middle fingers in the other two holes.

4. Stand four or five steps behind the start of the bowling lane.

Face towards the ten pins.

5. To bowl the ball, take four or five steps towards the start of the lane.

As you step up to the lane,
bring your arm back behind you
in a straight line.

6. At the start of the lane, swing your arm towards the pins.

When the ball is close to the floor, let it go and roll it towards the pins.

Your feet mustn't go over the line at the start of the lane.

Look at the pins as you let go of the ball.

Try to roll the ball down the middle of the lane. If the ball goes too far to one side of the lane, it won't hit any pins.

7. Watch the ball as it rolls down the lane. A computer will count how many pins you knock over.

If you knock over all ten pins, this is called a **strike**.

Some of the pins might wobble without falling over!

8. A **conveyor belt** will bring your ball back to you.
You might not knock over all the pins
the first time.
Bowl again to try to hit the pins you missed!

The conveyor belt brings your ball back.

9. After you have had your turn, the machine at the end of the lane will put down ten new pins. Move away from the lane so the next player can have a turn.

The machine at the end of the lane puts down new pins.

10. After everyone has had their turn, play again. Each person gets to bowl ten times.

At the end of the game, the player who has knocked over the most pins is the winner!

Glossary

conveyor belt *(noun)*
a machine with a moving band that carries things from one place to another

lane *(noun)* the long, shiny floor where the ball is bowled

pins *(noun)* small pieces of wood that are shaped like bottles

strike *(noun)* when all ten pins are knocked over with one ball